PUFFIN

Sheltie the Shetland Pony

Make friends with

The little pony with the big heart

Sheltie is the lovable little Shetland pony with a big personality. He is cheeky, full of fun and has a heart of gold. His best friend and new owner is Emma, and together they have lots of exciting adventures.

Share Sheltie and Emma's adventures in

SHELTIE AND THE RUNAWAY
SHELTIE IN DANGER
SHELTIE RIDES TO WIN
SHELTIE LEADS THE WAY
SHELTIE AND THE STRAY
SHELTIE AND THE SNOW PONY
SHELTIE FOR EVER
SHELTIE GOES TO SCHOOL
SHELTIE IN DOUBLE TROUBLE
SHELTIE AND THE FOAL
SHELTIE RACES ON

Peter Clover was born and went to school in London. He was a storyboard artist and illustrator before he began to put words to his pictures. He enjoys painting, travelling, cooking and keeping fit, and lives on the coast in Somerset.

Sheltie and Emma have lots of fans. Here are some of their comments:

'I love reading Sheltie books so much because I like the ponies and their exciting adventures.'

'You can't put the Sheltie books down until you have finished them because they are so good.'

'Sheltie always gets up to mischief and it makes me feel excited and scared!'

'I think people learn a lot more about ponies when they read Sheltie books because they tell you a bit about how to look after them and also how fun they can be.'

Sheltie the Shetland Pony

Peter Clover

PUFFIN BOOKS

PUFFIN BOOKS

Published by the Penguin Group
Penguin Books Ltd, 80 Strand, London WC2R 0RL, England
Penguin Putnam Inc., 375 Hudson Street, New York, New York 10014, USA
Penguin Books Australia Ltd, 250 Camberwell Road, Camberwell, Victoria 3124, Australia
Penguin Books Canada Ltd, 10 Alcorn Avenue, Toronto, Ontario, Canada M4V 3B2
Penguin Books India (P) Ltd, 11 Community Centre, Panchsheel Park, New Delhi – 110 017, India
Penguin Books (NZ) Ltd, Cnr Rosedale and Airborne Roads, Albany, Auckland, New Zealand
Penguin Books (South Africa) (Pty) Ltd, 24 Sturdee Avenue, Rosebank 2196, South Africa

Penguin Books Ltd, Registered Offices: 80 Strand, London WC2R 0RL, England

www.penguin.com

Sheltie the Shetland Pony first published in Puffin Books 1996
Sheltie Saves the Day first published in Puffin Books 1996
This edition published 2002
8

Created by Working Partners Ltd, London W6 0HE

Typeset in 14/22 Palatino

Made and printed in England by Clays Ltd, St Ives plc

British Library Cataloguing in Publication Data
A CIP catalogue record for this book is available from the British Library

ISBN 0-141-31387-0

Contents

Sheltie the Shetland Pony

For Stephen and Missy

Chapter One

'I wish we didn't have to move house,' said Emma. 'And I wish we didn't have to go and live in the rotten countryside either!'

Dad raised an eyebrow behind his newspaper. Mum smiled and scraped butter on to a piece of toast for little Joshua.

'I bet everyone will be horrible,' moaned Emma. She poured some milk into her cereal bowl. 'Why do we have to move anyway? It's nice here!'

Mum gave Emma a stern, no nonsense look.

'Because Daddy has a new job. And besides, it will be nice for you and your little brother to grow up with fresh air to breathe, and green fields to run and play in. You'll love it, Emma. Really you will. Just wait until you get there. It will be a new start for all of us. A real adventure. You'll simply love it.'

'I won't,' Emma muttered. She stuck out her bottom lip and made her face look even more unhappy. 'I'll hate it! I know I will.'

By lunchtime, everything was packed up and ready to go. It was a long drive to Little Applewood and it was almost dark by the time they arrived. It was too late to see or do anything, so they all went to bed early.

Next morning, Emma woke to a strange crowing sound.

What is that? Emma wondered, still half asleep. She rubbed her eyes and blinked at the unfamiliar surroundings.

Outside, the cockerel crowed again. Emma decided to investigate. She slipped out of bed and peered through the window of the funny little attic room that was her new bedroom.

It was a glorious sunny day. Emma could see green hills rolling far off into the distance, with cows and sheep grazing in the meadows. She saw a little stream, winding its way through an orchard of old apple trees. She saw a field of golden corn and a small paddock at the end of the garden.

Then Emma's eyes grew wide. In the paddock was a fat little Shetland pony. A very small horse no taller than Emma herself. It looked like a giant guinea-pig.

The pony was light chestnut

coloured and it was resting its fuzzy chin on the top bar of the wooden fence.

Emma got dressed and rushed downstairs. She couldn't find her shoes anywhere. There were boxes and packing cases all over the floor in every room. Emma found her green wellies and pulled them on at the back door.

Then she raced out into the garden.

A little path ran from the cottage door right down to the paddock. When the pony caught sight of Emma, it dashed round and round in a big circle.

Emma stood up on the bottom rung of the fence, resting her arms over the top bar. The pony trotted over to say hello. He pushed his soft, velvety muzzle into her hands.

'What a nice face you have,' said Emma. The pony's brown eyes twinkled beneath his big bushy mane.

Emma stroked his head and pushed her face closer for a better look. The pony seemed to be smiling. Emma threw her arms around his neck and snuggled in with a big hug. The pony just stood there as quiet as a lamb.

'I see you've already met Sheltie then,' called Mum, crossing the yard with a handful of fresh carrots. Emma spun round, jumping off the fence.

'He's lovely. Who does he belong to?' asked Emma.

Sheltie saw the carrots and did a mad lap of the paddock at lightning speed.

'He's yours if you want him to be,' said Mum, knowing already that Emma did. She fed Sheltie a carrot. The carrot disappeared in a flash.

'Sheltie belongs to Mrs Linney, who sold us the cottage,' said Mum. 'But she can't keep him in her new town flat, so he can stay here and live with us. Would you like that, Emma? Your very own pony.'

'Oh yes,' said Emma excitedly. 'I'd like that very much.'

Mum passed her a carrot and Emma laughed as it disappeared as quickly as the first.

'Will I be able to ride him?' asked Emma.

'Of course,' said Mum. 'He's just your size. And Mrs Linney is coming over this afternoon with Sheltie's tack. She's going to give you your very first riding lesson and tell you how to look after him.'

Chapter Two

Mrs Linney wasn't at all like Emma had imagined. She wasn't two metres tall and as thin as a pole. She was short and squidgy and round, like a dumpling. She wore scruffy clothes and green wellies like Emma.

Emma sat on the fence and watched Mrs Linney come plodding up the front path with a saddle and bridle slung over her arm. A tiny black riding hat for Emma sat perched on top of her head.

'Hello there! You must be Emma.'

Emma smiled. Then Sheltie nudged her in the small of her back and gently knocked her off the fence.

'Ow!' Emma laughed, and Sheltie shook his head, blowing and snorting. His eyes twinkled, full of fun and mischief.

Mrs Linney plopped the saddle over the top of the fence and ruffled Sheltie's long shaggy mane. Sheltie grabbed one of the buttons on Mrs Linney's cardigan between his teeth. He tried to pull her into the paddock, through the bars of the fence. Emma giggled.

'He's a real terror, isn't he, Emma?'

Mrs Linney pulled the cardigan free. Sheltie spat out the button on to the grass at her feet.

'You're going to have your hands full with this one,' said Mrs Linney, palming Sheltie a treat. 'You love your peppermints, don't you, Sheltie?' Sheltie's eyes sparkled.

Mum came out to watch as Mrs Linney saddled up Sheltie. He had short legs and a huge stomach that almost brushed the long grass. It was funny watching the leather girth being strapped round his fat belly. Sheltie kept nipping at Mrs Linney's bottom with his teeth every time she bent over, and tugging at her tweed skirt.

Mrs Linney was all smiles and good

humour. 'Now then. Let's get you up, Emma. You're not nervous, are you?'

'No,' said Emma. She was really, just a tiny bit, but she wasn't going to say anything. All the same, it felt very odd sitting up in the saddle on Sheltie's back. He was only a Shetland pony, but it seemed to Emma that she was rather a long way from the ground.

Mrs Linney showed Emma how to hold the reins, and how to position her feet in the stirrups.

'Toes up, heels down.'

Emma laughed and sat with a straight back and elbows tucked in, hands low.

'Perfect. A proper little horsewoman,' said Mrs Linney. That pleased Emma.

'Now, all we're going to do today is to walk on, nice and steady, with me holding the leading rein. Ready?'

'Hold on a minute,' called Dad, striding from the cottage with a camera. 'Say cheese.'

Emma grinned. Sheltie grinned too, or at least he appeared to. He really did have a funny, smiley look about him.

Mrs Linney led Sheltie around the paddock in a gentle circle. Sheltie was on his best behaviour. Emma's grin spread until the corners of her mouth almost touched her ears.

'Well done, Emma,' said Mum, clapping her hands. Mrs Linney

walked alongside as Emma and Sheltie circled the paddock.

'Am I good?' asked Emma.

'You're wonderful,' said Mrs Linney.

Emma leant forward to pat Sheltie's hairy neck. 'You're the best pony in the whole world,' she whispered in his ear.

'There's no doubt about it,' said Mum. 'Those two are going to be the very best of friends.'

'Walk on,' called Emma. 'Walk on.'

Chapter Three

After Emma's riding lesson, Mrs Linney came into the cottage for a cup of tea. They all sat at the kitchen table as Mum passed round the biscuits.

'Always remember to bolt the paddock gate properly,' said Mrs Linney, 'otherwise Sheltie will open it. He's a very clever pony.'

At that moment, Sheltie trotted right in through the open kitchen door. He skidded across the floor tiles with a clatter of hooves. He went straight for the table and lunged at the sugar bowl, knocking the milk jug flying. Mrs Linney fell off her chair with a bump.

Before anyone could stop him, Sheltie was crunching a mouthful of sugar cubes.

'Sheltie, you naughty boy!' Mrs Linney pulled herself to her feet.

'Always remember to bolt the paddock gate properly,' said Mum with a laugh. Emma giggled.

'Come on, Sheltie.' Mrs Linney led the way outside. 'As you can see, Sheltie's a very determined pony. There's not much he can't do. Opening gates is his speciality.'

They took Sheltie back to the paddock. Mrs Linney showed Emma how to lock the gate properly, and how to fit the little pin in place to prevent Sheltie sliding the bolt across.

Sheltie was frisky, and watched all this with great interest.

At the far end of the paddock was a little shelter made of stone. It looked like a little house.

'This is Sheltie's field shelter,' said Mrs Linney.

Emma rushed inside. Sheltie followed, looking very pleased with himself. Inside, on the back wall, was a feeding manger.

'This is for Sheltie's pony mix. One small scoop a day. And this rack is for Sheltie's hay.'

Outside, Mrs Linney showed Emma how to fill the water trough from a rubber hosepipe fixed to the wall. Sheltie stuck his head in the trough and blew bubbles. Then he tried to drink the water straight from the hose. Emma got soaked, but she didn't mind.

'There's plenty of grass in the paddock for Sheltie to graze,' said Mrs Linney. 'So you only need to feed him once a day.' Sheltie shook his head from side to side, whipping both of his cheeks with his long mane.

Emma thought having a pony of her very own to look after was going to be great fun. Living in the country wasn't so bad after all.

Every evening, when Emma said goodnight, Sheltie would follow her to the gate and watch her walk up the garden path to the cottage. And the very first thing Emma did each morning when she woke, was to look out from her bedroom window to see Sheltie standing by the fence, waiting for her with a twinkle in his eye.

Sheltie was Emma's very best friend.

It wasn't long before Emma could ride all by herself.

One day, Mrs Linney came over and led Sheltie and Emma down to the end of the lane at the side of the cottage.

Halfway down the lane, behind a stone wall, sat another cottage. The cottage garden wasn't filled with flowers like Emma's garden. It was a vegetable garden.

Sitting up in the saddle, Emma could see right over the wall. She saw rows and rows of cabbages planted in neat, straight lines. She saw runner beans climbing up long bamboo canes. And green feathery carrot tops sprouting from the freshly dug earth. She saw

onions too, and leeks, all planted out beautifully in carefully arranged rows.

As Sheltie and Emma passed by, an old man's head popped up from behind the wall.

'Good morning, Mr Crock,' said Mrs Linney.

'Bahh!' grunted the old man. Then he ducked down again, behind the wall.

Emma turned her head right round and stared at the man.

'Don't take any notice of him, Emma,' smiled Mrs Linney. 'He's just an old grump who cares about nothing but his precious vegetables.' Sheltie stuck his nose up in the air and plodded on.

At the end of the lane they turned around.

'Right then,' said Mrs Linney. 'Off you go.' Emma was going to ride back down the lane to the paddock, all on her own.

Emma was a bit nervous, but proud and excited at the same time. She patted Sheltie's neck, then squeezed with her heels.

'Walk on, Sheltie, walk on.'

Sheltie was very good. He walked at a slow pace down the lane. He seemed to know that Emma's first ride was very special.

Sheltie was on his best behaviour . . . until they came back to Mr Crock's vegetable garden!

Chapter Four

Suddenly, Sheltie stopped. Emma kicked her heels, but Sheltie just stood there, peering over the wall into Mr Crock's vegetable garden.

'Walk on, Sheltie. Walk on,' called Emma. But Sheltie just rested his head on the stone wall. His nostrils twitched as he smelt the fresh carrot tops and cabbages.

Mr Crock popped up from behind

the wall, all angry and grumpy.

'Gerroff!' he snapped. 'Go on, get out of here. And keep that filthy pony away from my vegetables.'

Emma's heart thumped in her chest. 'Walk on, Sheltie. Walk on.'

'Scram!' yelled Mr Crock, and Sheltie flew. Emma held on tight, as Sheltie bolted all the way back to the paddock. When they got to the gate, Sheltie slowed down to a walk.

'Well done,' called Mum. Little Joshua waved and clapped his hands.

Sheltie trotted over, looking for a treat.

'There was a nasty man,' said Emma. 'He called Sheltie a filthy pony.'

'Just ignore him,' said Mrs Linney,

coming up the path. 'He's just a grumpy old man. Just because the summer fête is only two weeks away, he thinks everyone is after his prize-winning vegetables.'

'I don't want his rotten old vegetables,' said Emma.

'No,' smiled Mum, 'but he probably thinks Sheltie does.'

'But you don't, do you, Sheltie?'

Of course, Sheltie said nothing. But there was a mischievous look in his eyes. And Emma was sure that all Sheltie could think of was those lovely juicy carrots and cabbages.

The next day it rained. Dark clouds filled the sky and it poured and poured. Sheltie didn't mind the rain, but Emma couldn't ride him that morning. Instead, Mum drove Emma into town to buy her a new school uniform.

'Yuck!' said Emma. She wasn't looking forward to starting her new school. She wanted to stay at home with Sheltie.

Emma sat in the front seat of the car next to Mum. Little Joshua sat in the back, strapped safely into his booster seat. Sheltie watched the car glide down the lane and out of sight. He gave a loud snort and shook the rain from his shaggy mane. Then he stamped his hooves. Sheltie wanted to go with Emma. He looked around the empty paddock, then trotted over to the gate. He began to think of those juicy carrots and cabbages in Mr Crock's vegetable garden.

Sheltie stood at the gate and looked down at the bolt. He had watched Emma open and close it many times. First Sheltie nudged it with his muzzle, but nothing happened. Then he took the little pin between his teeth and pulled. The rest was easy-peasy. Sheltie pushed the bolt across and nudged open the gate.

Sheltie felt very pleased with himself and gave a loud blow. The rain stopped and the sun began to shine as Sheltie trotted up the lane, splashing through the puddles.

Mr Crock was busy in the potting shed. He didn't see Sheltie push open the garden gate. Sheltie looked up and down the neat rows of vegetables and sniffed the air. The vegetables smelt lovely.

Sheltie put his head down and pulled a huge carrot out of the damp earth. The carrot was very juicy and very crunchy. Sheltie thought it tasted delicious. Then he tried a cabbage. That was good too.

Sheltie was eating his second

cabbage when Mr Crock came out of the potting shed. Mr Crock's face turned to thunder when he saw Sheltie standing in the middle of his precious vegetables.

'Scram!' he yelled at the top of his voice. Sheltie jumped, and ran away as fast as he could. He tore through the gate and back down the lane to his paddock.

Emma's dad was in the kitchen, pouring himself a cup of tea. Mr Crock burst in through the back door hollering and shouting.

'That animal of yours has been in my garden, stealing my cabbages.' Mr Crock sounded furious. 'I won't stand for it,' he said. 'If you don't keep that pony away from my vegetables, I'll call the police and have them take him away!' Then, before Dad could say a word, Mr Crock stormed off in a huff.

Chapter Five

When Emma came home, Sheltie was hiding in his field shelter. Dad had fitted the paddock gate with a padlock and chain. He told Emma what had happened and said that the paddock gate must be kept locked at all times. He showed Emma how to use the padlock and the key. Poor Sheltie was in disgrace.

'What a lot of fuss over a few

cabbages,' said Mum. But Sheltie had been naughty and it was wrong of him to steal Mr Crock's vegetables.

The next day, Mum baked a nice apple pie, and Emma wrote an apology to Mr Crock in her best handwriting. Together they took the pie and the letter along to grumpy old Mr Crock.

Mr Crock wasn't pleased to see them.

But he took the apple pie all the same and grunted when Emma handed him the apology.

'Just keep that pony out of my garden,' said Mr Crock. 'I don't like ponies. And I don't like them eating my cabbages. Like I said before, if I catch him again I'll call the police and have them take him away.' Then he stomped off into his potting shed.

Emma bit her bottom lip and was close to tears.

'Can Mr Crock really make the police take Sheltie away?' asked Emma.

'I don't expect so,' said Mum. 'But we'll keep an eye on him all the same.'

Emma was very worried. All day long she kept rushing to the paddock gate to check the padlock and make sure it was locked. It always was.

Emma wore the key around her neck on a piece of string. Sheltie was very frisky. He thought this was a new game and kept trotting over to the gate to nibble at the new lock and chain.

Two days later, Mr Crock arrived at Emma's cottage with a policeman. There was a sharp knock on the door. Mr Crock stood in the doorway. Emma's mum looked surprised. Dad looked puzzled.

'That pony of yours has been at my cabbages again,' said Mr Crock. 'I warned you what would happen if you didn't keep him out of my garden.' His face looked angry and mean. 'That pony is a thief!'

The policeman gave Emma a polite smile. He couldn't believe Mr Crock was making all this fuss over a few vegetables.

'But that's impossible!' cried Emma. 'Sheltie's gate is locked and I have the key right here.' She dangled the key from the piece of string for the policeman to see.

'Well, miss, two more cabbages have gone missing. And Mr Crock here says it must be your pony.'

They all went outside and down to Sheltie's paddock. The chain and padlock were firmly in place, and the gate was locked and bolted. Just as Emma had left it.

The policeman walked around the paddock looking for any broken fencing. Sheltie followed the policeman, tossing his head. He thought this was another new game.

'Well, Mr Crock,' said the policeman, 'there doesn't seem to be any way that this pony could have possibly escaped. I'm afraid there is nothing I can do.' The policeman smiled and gave Emma a pat on the head.

'What about all the hoof prints then?' said Mr Crock. 'That proves it, doesn't it? Come and take a look.' They all marched up the lane to look at the hoof prints.

They were there all right. Lots of them. All over the muddy earth. Emma bent down and pressed her hand into one of the hoof marks. She stretched out her fingers wide.

'These can't be Sheltie's hoof prints,' said Emma. 'They're far too big. Sheltie has only little hoofs.'

The grown-ups stood and stared.

Emma was right. The hoof prints were far too big to be Sheltie's.

'Bahh!' said Mr Crock. 'Just keep that pony away, that's all.' And he stomped off into his cottage.

That evening, Emma said goodnight to Sheltie and went to bed.

Sheltie stood with his fuzzy chin over the wooden fence. The little pony watched the moon come up over the cottage roof. And as it grew dark, he watched the stars come out one by one.

When the last light shining from the cottage went out, Sheltie trotted into his stable. He stood looking out into the paddock.

Sheltie was wide awake.

In the darkness of the shadows, Sheltie saw someone walking along. His ears pricked up as he watched a strange figure pass by the cottage and continue down the lane.

Sheltie gave a blow and shook his mane. He trotted over to the far end of the paddock for a better look. His keen eyes peered into the darkness, watching the dark figure disappear down the lane and into the night.

Chapter Six

The next day, when Mr Crock went into his vegetable garden to count the cabbages, he found another two had gone missing.

'Right. That does it!' said Mr Crock. And he went about setting a trap.

Mr Crock tied a length of washing line across the cabbage patch. The line was just above the ground and pulled very tight. On the end of the line,

Mr Crock fastened three tin cans. Then he stood back with his hands on his hips and admired his work. He jiggled the line with his foot and the tin cans rattled. Mr Crock smiled. If anyone tried to walk through those cabbages now, he was going to know about it.

That night, Mr Crock stayed awake. He sat in his potting shed, waiting. He waited until the moon came out and the sky grew dark. He waited and waited until everyone in Little Applewood was fast asleep.

Just after midnight, Mr Crock heard a noise. He cocked his head to one side, and listened. The tin cans were rattling. There was someone in the vegetable garden!

Mr Crock dashed out of the potting shed, waving a garden rake and shining a torch. But when he got to his cabbage patch, there was no one to be seen. Whoever it was had run away. Mr Crock shone his torch along the rows of vegetables. Two more of his cabbages were gone!

Emma had been up for ages. It was another lovely sunny morning. She filled Sheltie's water trough and gave him his pony mix. One small scoop, just like Mrs Linney had said. And one tiny handful extra, for luck. That was Emma's idea.

Today, Sheltie and Emma were going to practise jumping. Emma could ride really well now. Most days, Emma rode

Sheltie across Mr Brown's field to Horseshoe Pond. There was a fallen log there that one day Emma was determined to jump. But first she had to practise.

The little jump Emma made in the paddock was six bricks high now. Emma set up the jump and placed the plank of wood across the bricks.

Sheltie was tacked up and eager to show off. He pranced around with a light, airy step lifting his feet high and blowing through his nostrils. His eyes twinkled as Emma mounted and settled herself in the saddle.

Mum came out of the cottage with little Joshua in her arms. Joshua loved to watch Emma and Sheltie riding around the paddock. One day, when he was big enough, Joshua was going to ride Sheltie too.

Sheltie trotted around the paddock in a wide circle, then approached the jump at a canter. Emma squeezed her

heels. Up and over he flew, like a bird. Joshua clapped his hands.

'Well done, Emma!' called Mum. 'Well done, Sheltie!'

Sheltie shook his mane and looked very pleased with himself. They turned around and took the jump again.

Then Sheltie suddenly looked round and nearly pulled the reins from Emma's hands. He stared across to the far end of the paddock and made funny snorting sounds. Emma glanced around to see what Sheltie was interested in. She saw Mr Crock peeping over the fence.

Seeing Mr Crock made Emma nervous. She rode Sheltie over to where Mum and Joshua were standing. Mum held out a carrot for Sheltie, but Sheltie was more interested in Mr Crock.

Mum looked over to where Mr Crock was standing and gave him a friendly wave. Mr Crock turned sharply on his heels and stomped off back down the lane.

'What a nasty man,' said Emma. 'Spying on us like that!'

'Don't take any notice, Emma,' said Mum. 'You just practise your jumping and make sure you lock the gate after you.'

Emma patted the key hanging from the string around her neck. 'I'll never forget, Mum. I promise.'

Chapter Seven

When Mr Crock arrived back in his garden, he set about making another trap. He made a wire snare and laid it carefully among the rows of cabbages. Then he hid the trap with a scattering of fallen leaves.

That night, Mr Crock stayed up late again. He hid in his potting shed and waited.

The sun went down and the moon

came up. The night sky twinkled with stars and the shadows outside grew long and black.

Sheltie stood alone in the paddock with his chin resting on the wooden fence. He looked up the garden path and watched the lights in the cottage go out, one by one.

Then Sheltie's ears pricked up. Someone was hurrying down the lane again, towards Mr Crock's cottage. Sheltie swished his tail and trotted to the end of the paddock. He saw a man disappear down the dark, leafy lane into the shadows.

Sheltie nudged at the top bar of the fence with his nose. The bar was loose and wobbled a little. Sheltie nudged it again. This time the bar creaked and moved a little more. Then Sheltie gave the bar a good hard push. The bar came away and fell on to the grass.

The second bar was much lower. It couldn't have been more than six bricks high from the ground. Sheltie turned and moved a few steps away. Then he trotted forward and jumped clean over it.

Sheltie trotted down the dark lane after the man. His long shaggy mane flew behind him, shining silver in the moonlight.

Overhead, an owl hooted in the treetops and Sheltie stopped in his tracks. He watched the man go through Mr Crock's gate and into his vegetable garden. Sheltie followed and stood in the shadows of the apple trees. From his hiding place, Sheltie watched the man making marks in the earth with a funny stick. On the end of the stick was a horseshoe. Then the man bent down and pulled two cabbages clean out of the soil.

Sheltie shook his mane.

The man hollered as his foot became trapped in the wire snare. Sheltie heard the rattling of tin cans as Mr Crock came rushing out of the potting shed. The thief ran away just before Mr Crock arrived.

Mr Crock shone his torch into the shadows. Sheltie stood frozen to the spot, caught in the beam of Mr Crock's torch.

'Aha! Just as I thought!' shouted Mr Crock. 'Caught you red-handed.' He walked up to Sheltie and grabbed a handful of the pony's mane in his fist. Sheltie didn't move. He stood there as quiet as a lamb as Mr Crock tied him to a tree.

'Now then,' said Mr Crock. 'Let's see what the police have got to say about this!'

The next morning, when Emma woke, she looked out through her little bedroom window and gasped. There was no sign of Sheltie anywhere. The paddock was empty!

Emma hurried downstairs just as the telephone rang. Mum answered the call. It was Police Constable Green. He said that Mr Crock had caught Sheltie in his vegetable garden stealing his cabbages. Could they come as quickly as possible? Emma started to cry. And Joshua, seeing his sister upset, began to cry too.

Dad threw on his jacket and hurried down the lane. Mum carried Joshua and held Emma's hand. They followed on behind.

PC Green stood with Mr Crock in the vegetable garden. Sheltie looked very unhappy. He was still tied to the tree.

When the little pony saw Emma he began to paw the ground. He shook his head and flicked his tail.

'Oh, poor Sheltie,' cried Emma. She wanted to run to him. But Mum held on tightly to her hand. The tears ran from Emma's eyes in a great flood. Joshua sniffed and buried his head in Mum's shoulder.

'Mr Crock here,' PC Green began in a very stern voice, 'was disturbed last night by a noise in his garden. On investigating the noise, he caught your pony in the act of theft.'

Emma's dad was standing among the remaining cabbages. Suddenly, Dad looked down and saw a long stick. On the end of the stick was fixed a horseshoe. He bent down to pick it up.

Then he saw the snare. And caught in the wire hoop was an old wellington boot!

'What's this then?' said Dad. He held up the stick and the boot for everyone to see. 'Looks like there was someone else here last night besides poor Sheltie.'

Mr Crock went very quiet. PC Green took the stick and the boot to examine them. First, he studied the horseshoe and matched them to the hoof prints in the soil. Then he studied the boot.

'Whoever lost this boot,' said the policeman, 'was using this stick to make hoof marks.'

'And whoever did that,' said Dad, 'is the thief who has been stealing your cabbages, Mr Crock.'

'And trying to make it look like Sheltie,' added Mum.

Emma broke free and ran over to Sheltie. She threw her arms around his neck.

'I knew it wasn't you, Sheltie. I just knew it.'

Mr Crock grunted. He knew Emma was right. Sheltie wasn't the thief after all. But the little pony was the only one who knew who the cabbage thief was.

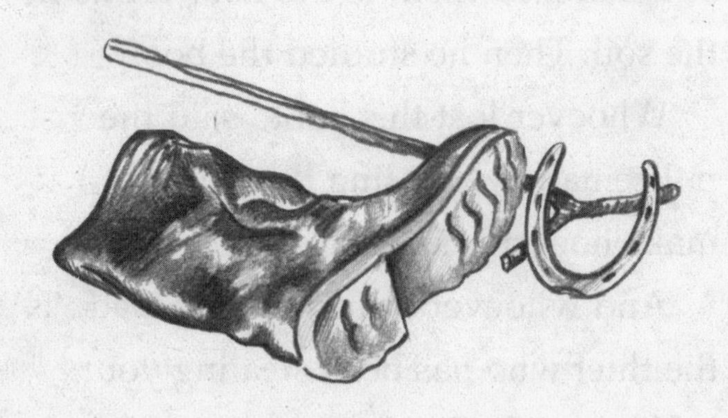

Chapter Eight

Later that afternoon, Mrs Linney came visiting. She said that everyone in Little Applewood was talking about Mr Crock and his missing cabbages. Old Fred Berry had seemed very pleased at the news. He had told Mrs Linney that perhaps now someone else would have a chance to win the special Cabbage Cup at the summer fête.

Fred Berry had been Mr Crock's best

friend until one day they'd had an argument. That was over ten years ago and they hadn't spoken since. In fact they were now the worst of enemies.

Emma was still very upset. Dad was in the paddock fixing the rail back on to the fence. Emma was in the paddock too. She was giving Sheltie a good brush. It wasn't much use though. Sheltie's coat was so thick and hairy. All the brushing in the world didn't seem to make any difference. But Emma liked to do it and Sheltie enjoyed the attention. At least Emma managed to brush all the mud off Sheltie's legs.

The sun was shining now and all the clouds had disappeared.

When Emma saw Mrs Linney

coming into the paddock she smiled and gave a little wave. Mrs Linney tried to cheer Emma up by talking about the summer fête.

'It's only a few days away now, Emma. It's a real treat. Everyone looks forward to it all year. There are stalls selling all sorts of things: home-made jam and cakes; pickles and bottled fruit; old toys and jumble. There are raffles for prizes, and hoopla and games and competitions. And there is a big tent where all the vegetables are judged to see who has grown the biggest and the best.'

Emma pulled a face when Mrs Linney mentioned vegetables.

'And there is a sheepdog trial,' Mrs Linney went on. 'All the farmers bring their dogs and try to round up sheep into a little pen. And there's a refreshment stall selling sandwiches, teas, coffees and fizzy pop. It's great fun, Emma. I bet you can hardly wait!'

Emma managed a weak smile.

'And don't forget Sheltie,' said Mrs Linney.

'Sheltie?' said Emma.

'Yes, Sheltie. Every year Sheltie gives rides to all the children. And you will be helping, won't you, Emma? You can lead Sheltie round the field. Sheltie loves it, don't you, Sheltie?'

Sheltie gave a nod and a loud blow. He remembered the peppermints he got every time he gave a ride. Sheltie became all frisky just thinking about it.

Emma said she would clean and

polish Sheltie's tack. She was proud of Sheltie and wanted him to look his very best.

Emma bit her bottom lip. 'Will Mr Crock be there?' she asked.

'Oh yes. He wouldn't miss the summer fête for anything. He's won the Cabbage Cup every year. But don't you worry, Emma,' said Mrs Linney. 'We'll all be there to keep Sheltie out of trouble.'

No more cabbages went missing over the next few days. Mr Crock had only six left and he kept guard over them night and day. On the morning of the summer fête, he picked them all and laid them carefully in a huge cardboard box. They were the size of big footballs.

Mum was busy making little cakes

for the food stall. Dad was in the big field helping to put up the tent for the vegetable show. And Emma was giving Sheltie one last brush. She was trying to comb all the knots out of his long mane. Sheltie just stood there as good as gold. He was looking forward to all those lovely peppermints.

At eleven o'clock, Dad came home for the cakes and took Joshua back with him to the fête. Mum followed later with Emma, leading Sheltie down the lane and through Farmer Brown's meadow to the big field. An enormous white tent stood in the middle of the grass. Lots of little stalls were set up all around it.

Across the field was an area marked off with ropes. In the middle of it was a small wooden pen. Inside the pen were six woolly sheep. Sheltie liked the sheep. He wanted to go over straight away to say hello. Emma had to keep hold of his reins to stop him wandering off.

One by one, the people started to arrive. Mrs Linney was there, wearing a big straw hat. She carried a shoulder bag to keep the money in that she would collect for Sheltie's rides. The summer fête was raising money to repair the village hall. Everything that was sold on the stalls would be contributed towards a new roof.

Little Joshua was holding a big slice of chocolate cake. He stood there eating it with chocolate all around his mouth. He offered a piece to Emma, and she gave a little piece to Sheltie.

Sheltie liked chocolate cake. But he liked peppermints more. He knew that Emma had lots of peppermints in her pocket and kept nudging and pushing at her anorak with his nose.

By twelve o'clock everyone in the village was there. Mr Crock arrived with his box of cabbages. He carried them inside the big tent and laid them out on the wooden tables, ready for the judging. His cabbages really did look magnificent. They were much bigger than any of the others.

The prizes and the special Cabbage Cup were displayed on a small table near the entrance. Mr Crock looked at the shiny, silver Cabbage Cup and smiled to himself. The judging for the prized Cabbage Cup was the highlight of the summer fête. When he came out of the tent, Emma tried to hide herself behind Mrs Linney.

'Good afternoon, Mr Crock,' said Mrs Linney.

Mr Crock touched his cap and grunted. Sheltie pawed the ground and gave a loud snort.

When Fred Berry arrived with a handcart full of cabbages, Sheltie became very restless. He blew and snorted and swished his tail.

'Good afternoon, Fred,' said Mrs Linney.

Fred Berry smiled. 'What a lovely day, Mrs Linney!'

Then he gave Sheltie a funny look and pushed his handcart into the big tent.

One of Fred Berry's cabbages was gigantic. It was much bigger than all the others. And even bigger than any of

Mr Crock's. Fred laid it out carefully on the table with the others, next to a card with his name on it.

When he left the tent, Fred gave Emma a nice smile. Sheltie pawed at the grass with his hoof. Something was upsetting Sheltie, but Emma couldn't work it out.

Chapter Nine

A little boy came up to Emma. He held a fifty-pence piece in his hand and asked Emma for a ride on Sheltie. Mrs Linney took the money, put a riding hat on the boy and helped him up into the saddle.

Emma led Sheltie slowly around the big field. Sheltie behaved very well and walked at a steady pace. Emma was very proud of him. When the ride was over, Emma gave Sheltie a peppermint. Sheltie crushed it between his teeth with a loud crunch.

There were more children waiting for rides. Emma led them all around the field one after another.

'What a lovely pony,' said all the mums and dads. They patted Sheltie and laughed as he gobbled the peppermints.

Little Joshua had a ride. His face

beamed with a happy smile as he rode Sheltie around the field. Mum walked along next to him. Sheltie was extra careful and didn't bump or jog once. But when they passed Fred Berry, Sheltie's ears suddenly flattened and a funny look twinkled in his eyes.

When the time came for the judging of the vegetables, everyone made their way into the big tent. Emma stayed outside with Sheltie and watched from the entrance.

The judging for the Cabbage Cup began. Emma listened to the announcement over the loudspeaker. 'First prize and winner of this year's Cabbage Cup goes to Mr Fred Berry!'

Emma jumped back as Mr Crock stormed out of the tent.

'Bahh!' he said as he rushed past.

A big cheer came from inside the tent and Fred Berry appeared, holding the shiny Cabbage Cup above his head. Again, Sheltie's ears went back and a funny look appeared in his eyes.

Whatever is wrong? thought Emma.

The next event was the sheepdog trial. The sheep were released from their little wooden pen. And one by one, the dogs tried to round up all six sheep and get them back in the pen within two minutes.

Each farmer gave directions to his dog with a series of whistles. It was funny to watch. Little Joshua jumped up and down and tried to whistle. All he could manage was a loud raspberry.

The dogs worked very hard, running

here and there, up and down. Sometimes the sheep stayed together in a tight bunch, and sometimes they all ran off in different directions. Most of the dogs managed to get two or three sheep into the pen. But no one was able to round up any more than that.

The last dog in the competition was Mr Brown's black and white collie. He was very good and managed to get four sheep into the pen. Everyone cheered, and Mr Brown was very pleased.

Then a strange thing happened. While Emma was busy watching the sheep, Sheltie suddenly lurched forward. The reins slipped through Emma's hands. Then Sheltie ran off and trotted into the centre of the field.

The sheep were out of the pen again and stood quietly munching the long grass. Sheltie went to work. All on his own without any help from anyone, Sheltie trotted backwards and forwards rounding up the sheep one by one.

Emma watched as Sheltie gathered all the sheep together into a tight bunch and drove them straight into the enclosure. All six sheep were safely inside the little pen!

The crowd cheered and clapped. Even Mr Brown joined in. He waved his best cap round and round in the air.

Mrs Linney went to catch hold of Sheltie.

'Good boy, Sheltie, good boy.' She reached forward for the reins. But Sheltie wasn't going to be caught. He was having far too much fun! His eyes twinkled and he shook his long mane. Then he was off again.

Sheltie trotted away in a straight line, across the field and into the big tent. There was a loud crash as the naughty pony knocked the trophy table over.

The next table held all the cabbages. Sheltie took Fred Berry's prize winning cabbage in his teeth and ran out of the tent. Several hands tried to grab him, but Sheltie was too fast. Off he went, holding the cabbage up in front of him.

The cabbage was really huge. It was so big that Sheltie couldn't see properly. He ran straight through a line of little flags strung out across the field. The line snapped and all the flags became tangled around his neck.

Sheltie ran as fast as he could, trailing the line of flags behind him. He looked so funny that Emma started to laugh, even though Sheltie was being very naughty. Other people were

laughing too. Little Joshua was jumping up and down and pulling Mum along. PC Green and a whole crowd of people chased after Sheltie. But Sheltie didn't stop.

He ran right back across the field and out through the lower gate. The gate led on to a muddy path which wound its way up to the allotments. The allotments were little plots of land laid out in neat, tidy rows, where some of the villagers grew vegetables.

The farmers' dogs barked and ran ahead of the crowd. Everyone followed to see what Sheltie was up to. When Sheltie got to the allotments, he raced over to the potting sheds. He stood in front of one and kicked the wooden door with his hoof.

Chapter Ten

Dad was the first to reach Sheltie. He pulled the line of flags free from the pony's neck. Sheltie dropped the giant cabbage at the shed door and let out a loud whinny. Emma had never heard Sheltie make such a noise before. When PC Green and everyone else arrived Sheltie began to kick at the shed door again.

'That pony is a nuisance to everyone,'

said Mr Crock. He had followed Sheltie like everyone else. 'It ought to be locked away where it can't do any more damage!'

Sheltie began to kick at the door again.

'Stop it, Sheltie. Stop it at once,' said Dad.

But Sheltie wouldn't stop. Emma tried to pull Sheltie away but he wouldn't budge.

'There must be something in there,' said Mrs Linney. She peered through a tiny crack in the wooden door.

'Who owns this shed?' asked PC Green.

Fred Berry stepped forward, looking very guilty. He was holding the prized Cabbage Cup in his hands.

'I do,' he said. 'It's my potting shed.'

'And what's in there that could be upsetting the pony?' asked the policeman. Sheltie was very quiet now.

'Only some old tools, flowerpots and bits and bobs,' said Fred. Sheltie suddenly gave a loud whinny. Emma jumped back with a start.

'Would you mind unlocking the door, Mr Berry? So that we can take a look inside.'

Fred's face turned bright red.

'But there's nothing in there,' he said. 'Just a lot of old rubbish.'

'Then you won't mind unlocking it, will you?'

Fred Berry had no choice. He took a key from his jacket pocket and unlocked the door.

Everyone was gathered round, wondering what could possibly be in the shed to make Sheltie behave so strangely. PC Green went inside. Emma's dad followed.

'Well, well, well. And what's all this then?' said the policeman. Mr Crock pushed his way through and stood by the open door. He looked inside.

'My cabbages!' said Mr Crock. 'My stolen cabbages! I'd know them anywhere.' And there, sitting on a wooden bench at the back of the shed were seven enormous green cabbages. Mr Crock's prize vegetables.

On the floor in front of the bench was one old wellington boot. PC Green bent down and picked it up. It was exactly the same as the old boot found in Mr Crock's garden.

'And what have you got to say about all this, Mr Berry?' said the policeman.

Poor old Fred owned up to the theft.

'All right,' he said. 'I admit it. I stole the cabbages.'

'Thief!' snapped Mr Crock. 'Can't grow your own so you think you can steal mine.'

'Do you have an explanation, Mr Berry?' asked PC Green. Fred Berry lowered his head in shame.

'I stole them, because every year Old Crock wins the Cabbage Cup,' said Fred. 'His cabbages are always bigger and better than anyone else's. I wanted to win. Just for once. I wanted to win

the prize.' He held the Cabbage Cup close to his chest.

Emma felt sorry for Fred. Although Emma knew that stealing was wrong, Fred didn't seem to be a bad man.

Mrs Linney felt sorry for him too. 'I remember when you two used to be the very best of friends,' she said. 'All those years ago before your silly quarrel.'

Mr Crock remembered too.

'What you did was very wrong,' said the policeman.

'I know. And I'm truly sorry for all the fuss and trouble I've caused,' said Fred.

Suddenly, Emma spoke up. She was near to tears. 'You're just two silly old men,' she said. 'What you should do is shake hands and be friends again.'

PC Green raised an eyebrow. 'It may not be that simple, miss,' he said. 'After all, there has been a theft reported.'

Mr Crock stood there thinking. He didn't look so angry now. Emma thought he suddenly looked very sad.

'Bahh!' said Mr Crock. He stepped forward and snatched the cabbage from the policeman's hands. 'There's no need to arrest anyone,' he said. 'They're my cabbages. And if I don't mind Mr Berry taking them, then there's been no crime committed.'

The policeman looked puzzled.

'But you said they were stolen, Mr Crock.'

'I've changed my mind. I don't want anyone to get into trouble over something as silly as a cabbage. Let's

just say they went missing and now I've found them.'

'Oh, well done, Mr Crock,' said Emma.

Mr Crock shook Fred Berry's hand. 'Let's just forget this nasty business ever happened,' he said. Mr Crock gave Emma a smile. 'And I'm sorry for blaming your clever pony for stealing my cabbages.'

Sheltie tossed his head and snorted loudly.

'Well if you're sure, Mr Crock,' said the policeman, 'then there's been no real harm done.'

Fred Berry handed Mr Crock the shiny Cabbage Cup. 'I think this really belongs to you.' said Fred. 'After all it was your cabbage that won the prize.'

Mr Crock looked embarrassed.

'No, Fred,' he said. 'You keep it.'

'I know,' said Emma. 'Why don't you two work together, and next year grow the biggest cabbages Little Applewood has ever seen!'

Everyone agreed.

'What a good idea. The perfect solution,' said Dad. He was very proud of Emma. And everyone thought Sheltie was wonderful.

'Wasn't Sheltie clever?' said Emma. She gave him two peppermints as a special treat.

Mr Crock was very happy to have his old friend back, and everything had worked out fine. They all walked back to the tent in the big field to have sandwiches, tea and cakes.

But when they got there, they found that the sheep had eaten everything. All the sandwiches. All the cakes. And every single cabbage off the vegetable table! Everyone laughed, including Mr Crock. It was the first time anybody had seen him laugh in years.

It had been a really exciting afternoon. And the best summer fête ever. Sheltie was awarded a blue rosette for rounding up all six sheep in the sheepdog trial.

Emma was so proud. She pinned the rosette to Sheltie's bridle and stood next to him while Dad took a snapshot.

'Smile, Emma. Say cheese. And you too, Sheltie.'

Sheltie tossed his head and gave a funny grin. He really was a very special pony.

Sheltie Saves the Day

For Mum and Dad

Chapter One

That morning, Emma's mum and dad had decided to paint the wooden gate at the front of the cottage. Mum was busy with the sandpaper, rubbing the wooden posts smooth. Dad was stirring the paint and keeping an eye on little Joshua at the same time. Joshua kept trying to dip his fingers into the creamy white goo.

All three suddenly looked up

together, as Emma came racing up the lane on Sheltie, her little Shetland pony.

Dad smiled. 'Here comes the Lone Ranger,' he said. Mum laughed and Joshua jumped up and down, clapping his hands together. He very nearly kicked the pot of paint over.

Joshua always got excited when he saw Emma riding Sheltie. He thought Sheltie was a racehorse. And if Emma ever took Sheltie over a jump, Joshua's eyes would grow wide like saucers.

Emma and Sheltie came to a halt with a clatter of hooves on the gravel path. Mum jumped back, startled.

'Did you forget to put the brakes on, Emma?' said Mum.

Dad had never seen her in such a hurry before. Emma's face was all red.

She looked very angry and upset. She jumped out of the saddle and landed with a thud.

'Whatever is wrong?' asked Dad.

'It's Horseshoe Pond, Dad. It's awful,' said Emma.

'Horseshoe Pond isn't awful at all, Emma,' said Mum. 'It's beautiful.'

'I know,' said Emma. 'Horseshoe Pond *is* beautiful. That's why it's awful what they're going to do to it.'

'Who's *they*?' asked Mum. 'And what are *they* going to do?'

Sheltie began to snort and blow. He shook his long shaggy mane.

'Sheltie thinks it's awful too,' said Emma. 'Men are coming to fill in Horseshoe Pond. They're going to pull down all the trees and flatten Prickly

Thicket to make a rotten caravan park! It's awful, Mum.'

'Surely not,' said Dad. 'Horseshoe Pond is on Mr Brown's farm. Mr Brown would never let a thing like that happen. A caravan park. I don't think so, Emma.'

'But it's true, isn't it, Sheltie?' said Emma.

Sheltie scraped at the gravel with his hoof. He always did that when he was trying to tell Emma something.

'I overheard Mrs Jenkins talking to the gardener. Mrs Jenkins said it was the worst news she had ever heard. And that she'd got it straight from the horse's mouth. But I don't know which horse it was that told her.'

Although it was a serious matter,

Mum smiled and said, 'That's only a saying, Emma. Horses don't really talk.'

'Well, Sheltie does,' said Emma. 'I understand everything he says. Don't I, Sheltie?'

Sheltie's eyes twinkled beneath his long mane. He nodded his head three times.

'See?' Emma said brightly. 'And Sheltie understands every word I say too. Don't you, Sheltie?'

The pony nodded again.

Joshua gurgled and squealed with laughter.

'Anyway,' said Emma. 'Sheltie isn't a horse. He's a Shetland pony. A very special Shetland pony.'

Emma threw her arms around Sheltie's neck and gave the little pony a big hug. Then she gave him one of his favourite peppermints. Sheltie loved peppermints.

Emma's dad went inside the cottage to telephone Mr Brown. He was going to ask the farmer if Emma's story was true.

Five minutes later when Dad came out again, his face looked grim.

'It's true, I'm afraid,' said Dad. 'Every word of it.'

Mr Brown was in trouble. Last year his tractor broke down and he was forced to borrow money to buy a new one.

This year he needed a new combine harvester. Without it he wouldn't be able to harvest his cornfields in the autumn.

Mr Brown needed money. And the only way he could get it was to sell off some of his land.

Two men were already interested in buying Horseshoe Pond and the big meadow. A little thicket of prickly holly bushes grew there too, and it was all going to be taken away.

'I don't think there's anything anyone

can do,' said Dad. Emma lowered her head and led Sheltie back to his paddock. She felt very sad.

Chapter Two

Horseshoe Pond was one of Emma's favourite places. The pond was in the shape of a horseshoe and where its two ends almost met and touched, there was a little hump of grass like an island. Emma liked to sit there and look out across the pond to the rolling hills, while Sheltie nibbled at the long grass.

There was a big sycamore tree which

grew on the island. Emma would sit beneath it and listen to the birds as she watched the fish and the dragonflies.

Emma would pretend that she was a princess or sometimes a pirate queen and that the island was her castle or pirate ship. And all the land as far as she could see belonged to her.

Emma couldn't imagine what Little Applewood would be like with no Horseshoe Pond and no magical island.

The next day, two men came in a jeep with shovels and spades. They put up a tent in Mr Brown's meadow and set up camp.

When Emma and Sheltie came trotting along, the two men were already busy at work. They were measuring things with a long tape and marking areas off all around the meadow with sticks and flags.

When the two men saw Emma and Sheltie, they both stopped and looked up. One of the men had black hair and a beard. The other man's hair was bright red and curly. Emma didn't like the look of them. Neither did Sheltie.

When Emma said 'Good morning', the two men just stared. The man with the beard spoke.

'And where do you think you're going, miss?'

'Horseshoe Pond,' said Emma. 'I always go there and sit under the tree.'

'Well, not any more you don't,' said the man. 'You're not to come anywhere near here.'

Sheltie gave a loud blow from his

nostrils. Emma didn't like the way the man spoke. Then she heard a voice behind her.

'Emma can come here as often as she likes.' It was Mr Brown. He ruffled Sheltie's long mane as he spoke. 'Don't you take any notice, Emma. The meadow hasn't been sold yet. It still belongs to me. I've only given these men permission to take measurements and make some tests before the sale goes through. In the mean time you can come here whenever you want.'

Mr Brown gave the two men a stern, no-nonsense look. They grumbled under their breath and stomped off over to their jeep.

Mr Brown turned and spoke to Emma. His voice was kind and filled with sadness.

'You can sit by the pond as long as you wish, Emma,' he said. 'Those men won't bother you.'

Emma gave a weak smile, then rode Sheltie over to the pond and jumped down from the saddle. Sheltie bent his head and nibbled on the fresh green shoots which grew there. Emma sat on the little island and watched Mr Brown walk back to the farm.

Emma didn't want to stay there for long because the two men kept looking over at her. But she felt that she should sit there for a little while because Mr Brown had been so kind.

Chapter Three

A few minutes later, the man with red hair came walking across the meadow. Emma's heart was beating fast.

'Hello,' said the man. He sounded friendly. 'I'm sorry if my friend was rude before, only we have a lot of work to do and we can't get on with it if there are too many people around.'

Emma didn't say anything. She

wished Mr Brown would come back. Sheltie stopped munching grass and looked up. His eyes shone, bright and alert. Emma noticed that the man was holding a piece of paper. The paper looked old and worn at the edges.

'What are you measuring?' asked Emma.

'Um, we're measuring for the drains,' said the man very quickly.

'And do you really have to fill in the pond?' asked Emma.

'Of course,' said the man. 'We can get at least three caravans where that pond is.'

Emma looked up through the leaves of the tree.

'Will you keep the tree?' asked Emma.

The man looked at the big sycamore

as though he had just seen it for the first time.

'It's only an old tree,' said the man. He waved the piece of paper towards Prickly Thicket. 'All those will be coming down too,' he said.

Suddenly, without warning, Sheltie lurched forward and snatched the piece of paper out of the man's hand. The man jumped, but Sheltie was very

quick and ran off across the meadow with the piece of paper in his mouth.

The man was very angry and yelled at Sheltie as he galloped away. Emma leapt to her feet.

'Sheltie, come back!' called Emma. But Sheltie took no notice. He was off, running back to his paddock as fast as he could.

The other man saw what had happened. He dropped the spade he was holding and tried to cut Sheltie off at the gate. But Sheltie reached the gate first and charged up the lane on his short little legs. The two men followed, huffing and puffing, with Emma running close behind.

When Sheltie reached the paddock, he flew into his little shelter at the end of the field. The two men were making a lot of noise. They were hollering and shouting so loudly that Dad came out of the cottage to see what all the fuss was about.

The two men were in the paddock, peering into Sheltie's field shelter. They were both shaking with rage as they watched a tiny corner of the paper disappear into Sheltie's mouth. With one gulp and a swallow it was gone.

'Oh, Sheltie. You naughty boy,' said Emma. But deep down inside, Emma was pleased. She didn't like the two men one little bit.

'What is going on?' asked Dad. The man with the black beard pointed to Sheltie. He jabbed at the air with his finger.

'That *thing* has eaten our document!'

Dad told the man to calm down and stop shouting. Mum had come out of the cottage now and came over to see what was going on. She held Emma's hand.

'He didn't mean to, honest,' said Emma. 'Sheltie's never done anything like that before. He's ever so sorry.'

Just then, PC Green, the village

policeman, came riding up the lane on his bicycle. He heard all the shouting and rode straight into the paddock.

When the two men saw the policeman they went very quiet.

'What seems to be the trouble?' said PC Green.

Emma told the policeman what Sheltie had done. She said that Sheltie was very sorry.

The policeman said that under the circumstances there was nothing that could be done and sent the two men away.

Chapter Four

That evening, when Mum came upstairs to say goodnight to Emma, Emma was lying in bed looking up at the pictures on her bedroom wall. They were pictures of Horseshoe Pond and the big sycamore tree which grew there. Emma had drawn them herself.

'I think Sheltie knows that those men are going to fill in the pond,' said

Emma. 'That's why he ate their silly piece of paper.'

Mum thought that perhaps Emma was right. She said goodnight and switched off the light.

All night long, Emma tossed and turned in her bed. She kept thinking of Horseshoe Pond and the new caravan park. She couldn't sleep a wink.

It was very late and dark when Emma heard Sheltie outside in his paddock. He was making funny whinnying noises. Emma got out of bed and looked out of the window.

In the moonlight she could see Sheltie standing by the fence. Emma looked beyond the paddock and out towards the meadow and Horseshoe Pond. In the daytime she could see the sycamore tree and just make out the water shimmering in the little pond. In the darkness Emma couldn't see a thing, but she looked all the same.

What is that? she thought. She looked hard. Emma could see a strange light moving around in the meadow. She stood at the window and watched the light in the meadow moving slowly to and fro.

Sheltie was still making funny noises and now he was pawing at the ground. Emma knew that Sheltie wanted to show her something. Emma decided to go and take a look. If she was quiet, then no one would ever know.

Emma got dressed and tiptoed downstairs. She unlocked the kitchen door and crept down the garden path.

When Sheltie saw her he gave a noisy blow and tossed his head.

'Shh, Sheltie!' Emma whispered as she unlocked the gate and went into the paddock.

Sheltie gave a little sneeze and urged Emma to follow him across to the far side of the field where a tall hedge separated the paddock from Mr Brown's meadow. The night was clear and warm. Emma looked up at the moon and stars twinkling in the sky. The moonlight made the hedge and all the grass shine silver.

Emma climbed up on to the bank using the twisted roots like a ladder. She stood with one foot on Sheltie's back to steady herself.

'Stand still, Sheltie,' said Emma.

'And stop fidgeting!'

Emma peered over the top of the hedge into the meadow. She could clearly see that it was the two men walking about. One of the men was shining a torch on the ground. The other man was holding a funny kind of stick. On the end of the stick close to the ground was a flat, round disc. It looked like a big frying pan with a very long handle.

The man was passing the frying pan slowly over the grass. A little light on the handle was flashing as he walked along. As Emma's eyes got used to the dark, she could see that the man with the frying pan was wearing headphones.

Every now and again the man stopped, and the other one marked the spot with a small yellow peg.

What are they doing? thought Emma. *And why are they doing it in the middle of the night*?

Whatever it was, she guessed it must be something secret. Something they didn't want Mr Brown or anyone to know about.

The next morning, Emma woke bright and early. She had a bowl of cereal for breakfast, then went outside to feed Sheltie. One scoop of pony mix plus one tiny handful for luck.

Normally, Sheltie would push his nose into the feeding manger before Emma had finished scooping. But today he just stood there and watched. He was blowing and snorting and stamping the ground.

'What is it, Sheltie?'

Emma was puzzled. Was he trying to tell her something?

Sheltie began scraping at the floor. As he pushed the hay aside, Emma noticed a piece of paper lying on the floor. It was the same paper that he had snatched from the two men the day before.

Sheltie hadn't eaten it after all! He

had been pretending and had only bitten off and swallowed one tiny corner.

Emma picked up the paper and held it in both hands. It was a map. An old drawing of Little Applewood. She recognized the meadow from the horseshoe shape of the pond. The sycamore tree and the thicket of shrubs and bushes were clearly marked.

Emma found her cottage on the map and traced her finger along the lane

down to the meadow. The farm was also marked and so was Fox Hall Manor. There were also lots of crosses drawn all over the paper. Emma counted them. There were at least twenty.

Emma turned the map over. On the back of the paper, printed at the very top in fine, fancy letters was a name and address. *Major Armstrong, Fox Hall Manor, Little Applewood, Chittlewink.* The map was scribbled on the back of old notepaper from the manor house.

Emma didn't know what to do. She thought it best to show Mum and Dad straight away. But Dad had already gone off to work, and Mum was busy in the kitchen, making posters for the local police force charity dinner.

Little Joshua sat at the table watching. Mum was trying to keep him out of the paint pots. His hands were already covered with sticky glue.

'Oh, Emma,' said Mum. 'Would you be an angel and take these cakes down the lane to Mr Crock for me? They're to say thank you for all those carrots he gave me the other day.' Six fairy cakes were packed into a little red tin on the table.

Emma put the map in the pocket of her jeans and took the cakes. She decided to show Mum the map later, when she wasn't so busy.

Chapter Five

Mr Crock was in his vegetable garden planting out turnips. Sheltie stuck his nose over the stone wall and blew a raspberry. When Mr Crock looked up and saw that it was Sheltie, he smiled.

'Hello, Emma,' he said. They had become good friends, and Mr Crock wasn't half as grumpy as he used to be. He thanked Emma for the cakes and asked if she would like one with a glass of homemade lemonade.

Emma followed Mr Crock through into the kitchen and watched him pour two drinks from a big jug. Sheltie looked in through the kitchen window. Emma had made him promise to be on his best behaviour.

As Emma ate her cake and drank her lemonade, she decided to show Mr Crock the map, and tell him all about the two men and their funny frying pan.

Mr Crock listened carefully to every word. Then he held the map and studied both sides of the paper.

'I think I know just what this is, Emma,' he said. 'Many years ago, before the old Major died, he started to worry that robbers might steal his valuables. So one day, the silly old fool gathered together all his treasures and took them out and buried them! He buried his treasure in some secret place, then forgot where he'd buried it.

'His family were very upset and searched everywhere, for part of the treasure that Major Armstrong had buried was the family collection of gold coins.

'There was a story that he'd drawn a map, but he couldn't remember where he'd put that either. No one ever found the map and the treasure was lost. The Major must have hidden the map in an old book or something.

'You know what I think this is, Emma? Major Armstrong's lost treasure map.'

'And those two men must have found it and are looking for the old Major's treasure!' said Emma.

Mr Crock told Emma that the men's funny frying pan was probably a metal detector.

'People use them to find metal objects such as coins buried beneath the ground.'

'What are we going to do?' asked Emma. 'Should we tell the police?'

Mr Crock thought hard for a moment. 'Perhaps it would be best for now if we didn't tell anyone, Emma. After all, those men haven't really done anything wrong. And we can't prove that they are looking for Major Armstrong's treasure, can we?'

'But if they do find it, I bet they'll use

the money to fill in Horseshoe Pond and build their rotten caravan park,' said Emma.

'Well, you'll just have to find it first,' said Mr Crock. 'Why don't you take a walk up to Horseshoe Pond and see what those two men are up to?'

When they went back outside, Sheltie was standing with his head in an apple tree, helping himself.

'Sheltie, you naughty boy!' said Emma.

'It's all right, Emma,' said Mr Crock. 'There are plenty of apples in that old tree. I don't suppose I'll miss one or two. But they're not very ripe yet. I hope Sheltie doesn't mind!'

Sheltie was full of mischief and pulled another apple from a branch of the tree.

'No, I don't think he minds at all,' said Emma.

Chapter Six

Emma rode Sheltie back down the lane to Mr Brown's meadow. When they got to Horseshoe Pond there was no sign of the two men, but there were small holes dug all over the meadow next to the little yellow pegs.

Emma glanced at her wristwatch. It was ten o'clock.

'They must still be asleep in their tent, Sheltie,' she said. 'I expect they're very tired if they've been up all night digging these holes.'

Sheltie looked at the holes and nodded. Then Emma had an idea.

'We'll come back nice and early tomorrow, Sheltie. And play a trick.' Emma chuckled to herself as they walked away.

In the afternoon, Emma gave Sheltie's coat a good brush. As she untangled all the knots in his long mane, Emma thought about Major Armstrong and his treasure. *Fancy not remembering where he'd buried it*, thought Emma. What a silly man he was!

Emma thought hard. She wondered where *she* would bury a secret treasure.

'I think I would bury it in a place where no one could see me digging,' she told Sheltie. 'Not out in an open meadow.'

Sheltie cocked his head to one side. He was listening carefully to every word that Emma said. Emma began to comb Sheltie's long tail. It was so long it almost touched the ground.

'I would bury it somewhere hidden away. Somewhere where people would never go.'

Then Emma thought of just the place. 'I know, Sheltie!'

The little pony's ears pricked up.

'I would bury it under the biggest holly bush in Prickly Thicket. No one would think of looking for it there.'

Sheltie nodded and sneezed. He thought Prickly Thicket would be the perfect place too.

The more that Emma thought about where she would bury the treasure, the more she wanted to go and take a look, just to see if old Major Armstrong himself had thought of that very same spot.

Emma decided to take Sheltie out for a ride. Prickly Thicket seemed just the place.

Emma knew that the men would be working in the meadow. But she thought that if she kept to the far side of the field, she could nip into Prickly Thicket without being seen.

It was three o'clock when Emma rode Sheltie along by the back fence of the meadow. The two men were there, just as Emma expected. They were still poking around with sticks and digging little holes where the yellow pegs were.

Emma rode Sheltie over as close to Prickly Thicket as she dared, then jumped down from the saddle and led the way into the bushes.

Sheltie stood on guard as Emma went to explore. But he quickly found a young shrub near by with green, tender leaves and was soon munching his way through it.

Emma picked up a long stick. There were lots of small trees and shrubs growing there as well as prickly holly bushes. Emma used the stick to brush the scratchy branches aside. There were stinging nettles too, so Emma had to be very careful. She made her way through the thicket to a big holly bush which she knew was there.

Emma stood before the big holly bush. It was covered with millions of prickly leaves and grew in a big round ball.

That's where I would bury the treasure! thought Emma. It would be very difficult for anyone trying to dig it up without getting scratched to pieces.

She walked around the bush then crouched down on the grass and peered beneath the lowest branches. There was a small gap on one side, like a secret opening which led into the middle of the giant bush. Emma crawled inside.

The prickly leaves pulled at her hair and caught on her sweatshirt. Emma pushed the branches aside with the stick. Then she prodded the stick ahead of her and poked at the ground.

The stick tapped against something solid. It was a rock. A large stone right in the centre of the bush.

Emma inched her way forward. The rock was the size of a football but flatter. A white cross was painted on top of the rock. The paint was grey and flaky in parts, but Emma could see the cross quite clearly.

Suddenly, a voice from behind her made Emma jump.

'What are you doing in there?'

Chapter Seven

Emma dropped the stick and crawled backwards out of the bush. The man with ginger hair stood looking down at her with his hands resting on his hips. Emma looked up slowly. She felt her face turning red.

'Nothing!' said Emma. 'I was just looking for mushrooms.'

'Mushrooms don't grown under holly bushes!' said the man.

'Sometimes they do,' said Emma. 'They grow all over this thicket.'

'Well, you'd better look somewhere else. We don't like kids messing around when we're working, and we want to come up here in a minute.' The man turned away and walked back to the jeep.

Emma rushed over to Sheltie and jumped into the saddle. In minutes, she was racing back down the lane to tell Mr Crock all about her discovery.

The next day, Mr Crock met Emma in the paddock bright and early. He carried a trowel and a large plastic carrier bag. Emma had just finished giving Sheltie his breakfast and was filling the water trough from the rubber hose.

'Here are the things you wanted, Emma. I can't come with you. I'm too busy. But you be careful and don't go getting yourself into trouble!'

It was eight o'clock when Emma and Sheltie disappeared up the lane.

When they got to the meadow the two men were nowhere to be seen. They were both fast asleep inside their tent, just as Emma had thought they would be.

'We must be very quiet, Sheltie,' Emma whispered.

She tiptoed over to some freshly dug holes. Then she made some new ones near by. Emma reached into the carrier bag and pulled out some old tin cans. She dropped them into the holes, then shovelled the earth back in. Sheltie

helped by pressing the soil down with his hooves.

'This will give that metal detector something to find,' chuckled Emma.

They buried all the tin cans as quickly as they could. Emma wondered what the men's faces would look like when they dug them up, thinking it was Major Armstrong's treasure.

They tiptoed past the tent again on the way to Prickly Thicket. Emma could hear the two men snoring inside. They were still fast asleep.

Emma led Sheltie to the big holly bush and showed him the opening in the side. Sheltie gave a loud snort and shook his mane.

'Now, make sure that you keep watch properly this time,' said Emma. Then she crawled inside the bush and ran her hand over the smooth stone with its white cross painted on the surface.

'Looks like we may have found something here all right, Sheltie,' said Emma.

Sheltie kept watch while Emma moved the stone and began digging.

Chapter Eight

Emma had only been digging for a little while when her trowel hit something solid with a dull 'clunk'. She pushed away the earth and uncovered a large metal box. The box had two rusty handles on each side and a big lock at the front.

It was about the size of a small suitcase and very heavy. Emma was so excited.

'It's the treasure, Sheltie! We've found Major Armstrong's treasure!'

Sheltie tossed his head and gave a loud snort.

Emma tried to drag the box out of the hole but it wouldn't budge.

'Goodness knows what's in here, Sheltie. It weighs a ton.'

Just then, Emma glanced behind her through a gap in the trees and bushes towards the meadow. She saw the two men coming out of the tent. They stood there, yawning and stretching their arms.

'Oh, Sheltie! The men have woken up,' said Emma.

When Sheltie looked over, both men were rubbing their eyes. They were still very sleepy and hadn't noticed Emma and Sheltie.

'We'd better hide this box again before they see us,' said Emma. She crawled back into the bush, then re-covered the box with earth and placed the stone back on top.

Sheltie stayed well out of sight until the treasure was buried again. Then, keeping very low, Emma led Sheltie through the bushes to the far side of Prickly Thicket. They followed the fence which ran along the back of the meadow, out of sight and away. The two men didn't notice a thing.

Emma's heart was thumping as they squeezed through a gap in the fence and joined the track which led back to the lane.

When they got to the paddock

Sheltie snorted and gave a loud blow as if to say 'That was a close one!'

Emma was so excited that she could hardly breathe. She looked down and saw that her clothes were covered in mud.

Mum came out of the kitchen and went down to the paddock with little Joshua bouncing along behind. When Joshua saw Emma's muddy jeans he clapped his hands together and laughed.

'What on earth have you been up to, Emma?' said Mum. 'You're filthy.'

Emma's shoes were muddy too and she had dirt all over her face and hands.

'Picking mushrooms,' Emma said quickly. She glanced at Sheltie. 'We've been looking for mushrooms in Mr Brown's back field.'

Mum noticed that they didn't have one single mushroom between them.

'You didn't have much luck then!' she said.

'No,' said Emma. 'Perhaps we'll be luckier tomorrow.'

Mum looked puzzled.

'What are you two up to?' she said.

'Nothing,' said Emma. Then she jumped back into the saddle and trotted out into the lane. 'I'm just popping up to see Mr Crock for a minute,' Emma called over her shoulder. 'I won't be long.'

Mum watched them disappear up the lane. Then she turned to Joshua.

'I'm sure those two are up to something!'

That night, when everyone was fast asleep, Emma got out of bed and stood by the window. She looked out into the darkness over to Horseshoe Pond.

Emma could see the lights moving about in the meadow again. She smiled to herself. She imagined the two men's faces as they dug up the old tin cans.

I bet they'll be really mad, she thought.

She could see Sheltie standing by the paddock fence and blew him a goodnight kiss.

See you in the morning, Sheltie. Tomorrow is Treasure Day!

Chapter Nine

Emma was up and dressed by half past seven. She pulled on her green wellies and went downstairs.

'My goodness, Emma,' said Dad. 'You're up early.'

Dad wasn't working today. He was going to make a start on Joshua's bedroom, stripping the old wallpaper off the walls. Mum was already busy at the kitchen table finishing her posters for the charity dinner.

'Where are you off to then?' said Mum.

'Sheltie and I are taking Mr Crock mushroom picking in Mr Brown's back meadow,' said Emma. 'We have to be there early to pick the best ones.'

'Well, we'll look forward to having mushrooms on toast for our lunch, won't we, Joshua?' said Dad. 'That is, if Sheltie doesn't eat them all first.'

Moments later, Mr Crock arrived pushing a wheelbarrow. Sheltie stood with his ears pricked up and blew Mr Crock a loud raspberry.

'Cheeky monkey,' growled Mr Crock.

'Morning, Mr Crock,' Mum said as

she wandered out into the yard. She smiled when she saw the wheelbarrow.

'Do you think you might fill the whole barrow? That would keep us all in mushrooms for years!'

'I thought I might as well collect some firewood while I'm at it,' said Mr Crock. 'No sense in wasting a trip to the thicket.'

'Well, good luck,' said Mum. She stood at the back door and watched as Emma and Sheltie led Mr Crock and his wheelbarrow up the lane.

It was still and almost quiet in Mr Brown's meadow. The two men were snoring soundly inside their tent, fast asleep.

As they pushed the wheelbarrow past the tent, Emma noticed a heap of old tin cans piled up by a number of freshly dug holes. Emma and Mr Crock looked at each other and exchanged a secret wink.

'I bet they were surprised when they dug that lot up!' whispered Emma.

They wheeled the barrow into Prickly Thicket. Sheltie led the way and pushed aside all the prickly branches. His coat was very thick so he didn't feel any of the scratchy twigs and leaves.

They parked the barrow next to the big holly bush. Inside the barrow was an old blanket. Mr Crock took the blanket and laid it on the grass. Then Emma took the small trowel and crawled into the bush.

It was much easier this time. Emma pushed the stone aside and shovelled

the loose earth away. Mr Crock kept watch through the trees, checking the tent across the other side of the meadow.

Emma tied a rope around Sheltie and attached the ends to one of the handles. Then Sheltie dragged the metal box out on to the grass.

Emma shovelled all the earth back into the empty hole and replaced the rock. She stood there with Sheltie and

Mr Crock looking down at the treasure chest.

'Best not to try and open it here,' said Mr Crock. 'Let's get it away safely and take it to PC Green. He'll know what to do.'

Mr Crock helped Emma to lift the box. It was very heavy, but they managed to load it into the wheelbarrow. Then Emma covered the box with the blanket.

'There, that's done,' said Mr Crock. 'Now all we have to do is get this barrow past that tent before those two sleepyheads wake up.'

Emma felt her heart sink in her chest. Her legs suddenly felt all wobbly. As she glanced over into the meadow she saw the two men standing by the tent!

Chapter Ten

The two men were both looking over towards Prickly Thicket.

'Oh no!' said Emma. 'They've seen us. They're coming over. What shall we do?'

Mr Crock began to pick up odd bits of branches and old twigs.

'Hurry, Emma. Pile as much firewood as you can into the barrow!'

They worked as fast as they could,

covering the blanket and treasure chest with dry twigs. Soon the wheelbarrow was piled high.

The two men strode into the thicket. The treasure chest and blanket were hidden from view. Well, almost.

'What are you two doing snooping around?' said the man with the black beard. He looked very angry and carried a big stick in his hand.

'We're not snooping around,' said Emma. 'We're collecting firewood. Mr Brown doesn't mind. It keeps the thicket clear and it's good wood for the burner.'

'Collecting firewood in the middle of the summer. Sounds a bit funny to me.'

'Not as funny as digging holes all over the meadow,' growled Mr Crock. 'What are you two up to anyway?'

'None of your business,' snapped the man. 'Now take that pony and that rotten old barrow out of here and be on your way. We've got important work to do!'

Emma and Mr Crock were only too happy to be on their way. Emma helped Mr Crock to lift the wheelbarrow handles and they started to push. But the barrow was very heavy and it took all of their strength to make it move.

'A bit heavy for a load of old twigs, isn't it?' said the man with the beard. 'Just what else have you got in there?'

The man with red hair glanced down at the wheelbarrow. He could see a corner of the blanket poking out at the side.

'What's this?' he said, reaching forward and grabbing the blanket. He gave it a hard tug and all the firewood fell off on to the grass. They all stood there, staring down at Major Armstrong's treasure chest.

'Well, well, well. And what have we here?' said the man with the black beard. He tapped on the metal box with his stick. 'Been doing a bit of digging on your own, have you?' he said. 'Seems like you two have found exactly what we've been looking for! Get some rope from the jeep, Red.'

Emma shouted, 'Run, Sheltie. Run!'

The man swung the stick but Sheltie was off, galloping away through the thicket.

'Hurry with that rope, Red. I'll keep these two here.'

Emma felt like crying. Tears welled in her eyes but she was determined to be brave.

The man pointed the stick at Mr Crock.

'Now you just behave yourself and keep quiet. And don't do anything stupid!'

Mr Crock stood with his hands at his sides. Emma's legs felt like jelly.

The other man came back with the rope and tied them up.

'Put them against that tree, Red,' said the man waving the stick.

Emma and Mr Crock sat beneath the tree with their hands and feet tied together.

'You won't get away with this,' said Mr Crock.

'I think we will,' said the man. 'It won't take us long to pack up our things and be on our way.'

'But we'll tell the police,' said Emma. 'And you won't be able to use the

treasure to buy the meadow or build your rotten caravan park.'

'We never planned to build a caravan park,' said the man. 'It was just an excuse to dig for the treasure. And now we've got what we came for and nobody is going to stop us!'

'You can't leave us here,' said Emma.

'I can do anything I want,' laughed

the man. 'And it's no use calling for help either. Mr Brown has gone out for the day, and the other houses are too far away for anyone to hear.' The man gave a horrible, mocking laugh.

'Don't worry, Emma,' said Mr Crock. 'Your mum will come looking for us when you don't turn up at the cottage for lunch.'

'And we'll be long gone,' laughed the two men. They each took a handle of the heavy metal box, and carried the treasure chest away. Emma and Mr Crock watched as the two men hurried to pack up all their things.

'Oh dear,' sighed Emma. 'What are we going to do now?'

Then she had an idea. Sheltie. Of course. He must be hiding somewhere.

Sheltie would know what to do. She took in a deep breath and called out at the top of her voice.

'SHELTIE!'

Chapter Eleven

Sheltie wasn't very far away. He was in the next field behind a hedge. The little pony's ears pricked up as he heard Emma's voice.

Sheltie cocked his head to one side, listening. He trotted out into the middle of the lane.

Something was wrong. Where was Emma?

Sheltie looked around. His nostrils

flared as he sniffed at the air. Then he galloped over to the fence as fast as he could and stuck his head over the top rail.

Sheltie looked up and down the meadow. He couldn't see Emma anywhere but he could see the two men. And they were coming out of Prickly Thicket carrying the metal box.

'SHELTIE!' Emma called again.

This time Sheltie knew that Emma was in trouble and needed help.

Sheltie gave his head a good shake and blew a loud snort. Then, eyes bright and alert, he galloped up the lane back to the cottage.

When he got there the front gate was locked. The gate had been fitted with a

new safety bolt to stop Joshua running out into the lane.

Sheltie looked at the bolt. It was just like the special bolt on his paddock gate. Sheltie saw the little pin which held the bolt in place and carefully pulled it free with his teeth. Then he slipped the bolt across and pushed the gate with his nose. Sheltie trotted round to the back of the cottage.

Police Constable Green's bicycle was propped up against the cottage wall. PC Green was inside collecting the posters Emma's mum had made.

Sheltie scraped at the kitchen door with his hoof. Emma's mum heard Sheltie outside and opened the door. Sheltie stamped his feet and pawed at the ground.

'What is it, Sheltie? Whatever's the matter?' said Mum. It was almost as if Sheltie was trying to tell her something. She stood at the open door and looked past the pony down the garden and into the empty paddock.

'Where's Emma?' said Mum. 'Is it Emma, Sheltie?'

Dad came out of the cottage with PC Green.

'What's going on?' said the policeman.

'It's Sheltie,' said Mum. 'He wants to show us something. I think Emma's in trouble.' She looked very worried. 'Go on then, Sheltie. Show us!'

Sheltie gave a loud snort and trotted off. He went a short way then stopped and looked back.

'We're coming,' said the policeman.

Sheltie set off again looking back

from time to time to make sure that Mum and the policeman were following. Dad had stayed behind to look after Joshua and watched from the front gate as Sheltie led the way.

Chapter Twelve

The two men had finished loading their jeep. Major Armstrong's treasure chest sat between them on the front seat and the engine was running ready for their getaway.

The jeep rolled forward just as Sheltie burst through the gate into the meadow.

Sheltie ran straight at the jeep at a flat-out gallop. The man with the black beard was driving.

Suddenly Sheltie stopped, right in front of the moving jeep. The brave little pony stood his ground as the jeep roared towards him.

Emma and Mr Crock could see what was going on from Prickly Thicket. Emma gasped as she realized that Sheltie wasn't going to move out of the way.

At the last moment the jeep swerved to go around Sheltie. The sudden turn made the front wheels stick in one of the freshly dug holes and the jeep's engine stalled. Emma breathed a sigh of relief.

Sheltie turned and kicked out with his strong back legs. He kicked as hard as he could. His hooves hit the side of the jeep with a loud thud and made two big dents in the driver's door.

The other door of the jeep flew open and the man with red hair jumped out and tried to run away. PC Green brought him down with a flying tackle and knocked the air right out of him. The man lay on the grass, unable to move.

Sheltie stood guard over him,

stamping his hooves just in case he decided to run off again.

The driver had hit his head when the jeep stopped so suddenly. He sat forward in his seat, dizzy and dazed.

PC Green pulled the door open and reached inside the jeep. He took the jeep's keys and handcuffed the man to the steering wheel.

'Over here! We're over here!' called Emma.

PC Green called the station on his police radio while Mum ran over to the thicket. She found Emma and Mr Crock tied up beneath the tree. She quickly undid the ropes.

'I knew Sheltie would bring help,' said Emma. 'I just knew it!' She blurted out the whole story to Mum.

'We found the treasure. Major Armstrong's treasure, and now we can save Horseshoe Pond!'

Mum gave Emma a big hug. She was so pleased to find that Emma was safe.

A police Range Rover pulled up in the lane and three policemen took the two men to the police station. Emma ran up to Sheltie and threw her arms

around his neck. Sheltie's eyes twinkled and he gave a loud snort.

'Oh, Sheltie, you're so clever,' said Emma. Mr Crock and PC Green agreed.

'You always know just what to do!' said Emma.

Sheltie pawed at the ground with his hoof.

Back at the cottage PC Green opened the big metal chest. The lock was all rusty and the box had to be opened with one of Dad's drills and a pair of pliers. Inside the box were Major Armstrong's treasures. The valuables he had buried all those years ago.

There were silver candlesticks, twelve silver goblets, a set of silver spoons, two little gold statues and all

of Major Armstrong's war medals. And in a big black velvet bag was the family's collection of old gold coins.

'This lot must be worth a fortune,' said the policeman. 'The Armstrongs will be very pleased to hear about this!'

And indeed they were.

Up at Fox Hall Manor the family were delighted to hear of Emma's find. They offered a big reward.

As the treasure was found on Mr Brown's land, Emma and Mr Crock thought it was only right that the reward should go towards helping the farmer and saving Horseshoe Pond.

There was enough reward money to help Mr Brown without him having to sell off one piece of land. Horseshoe Pond was going to stay exactly as it was. Little Applewood would remain a peaceful little village. Thanks to Emma and Sheltie!

That evening Emma went out to the paddock with a bagful of fresh carrots. Sheltie was frisky, tossing his head and swishing his tail. When he saw Emma with the carrots he ran over and snatched the whole bag out of her hands. Then he ran off around the paddock, carrots spilling everywhere.

Emma laughed. 'Oh, Sheltie, you *are* naughty sometimes. But you're the best pony in the whole wide world!'

Sheltie munched the carrots and blew a raspberry. He had to agree. He *was* the smartest little pony ever.